About the Author

James Douglas Leach was a WWII baby named after Douglas McArther on July 9th, 1943. Jim is a risk taker and likes to jump off a cliff and look for an umbrella on the way down. It has served him well. His success in the stock market and Bitcoin has been a pleasure.

This octogenarian says his accomplishments are due in large part to Cindy, his lovely and talented wife of 61 years. She would dress up in crazy costumes and entertain on their bus tours. She became a volunteer EMT first, and Jim followed her lead. They were on ambulance duty in Cheyenne County for ten years.

Jim's résumé of over-the-top life experiences is amazing. He farmed 7,000 acres of mostly rented land in Bird City, Kansas, and put 10,000 hours on his first tractor, a 900 Case. The lost art of straight driving became obsolete with GPS. This farm kid, now man, set the state record for the highest yield in sugar beet production in Kansas. He is an overachiever who likes hot cars and has raced five of the seven corvettes he has owned at the Wichita, KS, International Drag Strip. He is a competition ballroom dancer who plays the guitar and a six string gitjo. His favorite picture is with a live tiger in Moscow, Russia; two glasses of wine for liquid courage helped.

The author, Jim, has published ten books of poetry and short stories, writing his first poem in the second grade. A pool shark in high school, he still tries to enjoy the game, peering through trifocals. At 53 years of age, Jim quit farming, sold his machinery, kept his farmland, and looked forward to a new adventure. Wondering what he could do without a college education, a sudden dream appeared: to drive a 45-foot tour bus all over the U.S. This wish came to fruition when he and his wife launched Jim and Cindy's Tours in Wichita, Kansas. They never dreamed he would drive a bus 700,000 miles in the U.S. and they would be flying all over the world. Now, this couple has escorted 18,000 tourists on 530 trips to 148 international destinations including 500 airplane flights in the last 25 years.

Jim is clairvoyant and has what he calls divine interventions twice a week. His kids call him 1-900 Jim.

Cindy and Jim are Christians, and Jim has a renewed friendship with Jesus Christ after his seven-by-pass open heart surgery.

MR. FARMER BILL

By James Douglas Leach

Illustrated by Michael Meissner

JAMES DOUGLAS LEACH

Dedicated to the children of the world.

James Douglas Leach, a former farmer, has led an exhilarating, unusual lifestyle as an international traveler. He and his wife have escorted thousands of eager sightseers to destinations around the world. Processing a prolific and brilliant imagination, Jim lays out master compilations of poetry, prose, and experiences to share with you.

 facebook.com/jim.leach.16

Published by Book Publishing Pulse

Acknowledgements

Thank you to my wife Cindy, of 61 years (1964), for her spontaneous enthusiasm throughout my life!

To Gianna Scott and Megan Stull of Flamingo Ink for their patience and diligence in assembling the book for production.

TABLE OF CONTENTS

MR. FARMER BILL

Mr. Farmer Bill lives here, and he owns a tractor.
Isabel is the name he picked out for her.

Isabel is green, and her smokestack is black.
Bill's farm dog likes the tractor. His name is Jack.

Jack rides on the tractor with Mr. Farmer Bill.
This German Shepherd thinks it is quite a thrill.

Bill brings a large water jug so the dog can drink.
The exhaust fumes are strong, and they do stink.

PULLING A PLOW

Aunt Susie packs Bill with a sumptuous lunch.
She even sends a thermos of fruit punch.

Jack is very interested in Bill's meal.
The dog thinks that if Bill shares, this would be ideal.

Bill tosses Jack three peanut butter cookies.
The German Shepherd barks. He likes these goodies.

Behind the tractor, Bill is pulling a plow.
In the nearby pasture is a Charolais cow.

CHASING A BUNNY

Jack jumps from the tractor to chase a bunny.
The chase is on, and the scene is funny.

The dog now follows the tractor back and forth.
He is getting tired of walking south and north.

Bill stops and lets the big dog jump aboard.
The dog's face with its tongue out is to be adored.

The sun meets the horizon to end the day.
Bill heads for the barn going on the highway.

THE MILKING STATION

Aunt Susie feeds them, and they prepare for bed.
Jack gets to sleep with Bill in this small homestead.

When morning comes, it is time to milk the cow.
Large pigs live here, and they must feed the sow.

The cats gather around the milking station.
A squirt to each mouth gives total satisfaction.

Gathering eggs from the chicken house is fun.
Aunt Susie rings the dinner bell, and breakfast is done.

THE SUDDEN STOP

Today, Bill decides to ride the white horse.
The German Shepherd wants to follow, of course.

The frisky horse wants to race with the dog.
They suddenly stop to make way for a bullfrog.

The unusual pause throws Bill from the saddle.
He flies through the air, and a fence he does straddle.

It's been an exciting day. They head for the house.
On the way to the barn, Jack catches a mouse.

WHEAT HARVEST

It's time to pull the combine out. Wheat harvest is here.
They begin to rush. Kick it into high gear.

Sweep all the grain bins out and also the truck.
They wish for nice weather and need some good luck.

The fields of green wheat have ripened to gold.
The fun times at harvest never get old.

The combine cuts the wheat and waits for the truck to come.
The farmer is so happy he starts to hum.

THE FIRE

The combine loads the truck with beautiful grain.
It will be taken to town and put on a train.

The farmer sells the wheat and buys the dog dinner.
Jack thinks his owner, Bill, is a real winner.

The hot combine exhaust catches the wheat field on fire.
The raging flames spread to the combine's big tire.

Fire trucks are coming all the way from town.
The burning combine and truck have a complete meltdown.

THE BARN DANCE

The poor German Shepherd got his eyelashes burned.
Everyone was worried, but the dog seemed unconcerned.

Bill still had wheat to cut, so a new combine was bought.
Aunt Susie brought out soup she had simmered in the pot.

In three more days, the wheat had all been cut from the land.
To celebrate, a barn dance was planned with a live band.

The men wore their Stetsons and cowboy boots.
The lady's fancy dresses added to their attributes.

THE AUCTION BARN

Many farmers and their wives rode horses to the dance.
The horses showed off their special strutting prance.

One of the cowboys wore a five-gallon hat.
He was followed to the dance by an alley cat.

The next day, the dance floor was cleaned and swept.
Bill and his wife liked the farm to be well-kept.

Bill went to the auction barn to buy a goat.
It was cold that day, so he wore a leather coat.

THE BILLY GOAT

Goats eat grass and mow the farm. It started the day's events.
The goat jumped on top of Bill's car and gave it some dents.

Sometimes, goats are a bit unruly. Watch out.
If you don't let them eat glue from tin cans, they pout.

One day, Bill saw a mountain lion walking on the road.
The ground was white because it had just snowed.

She was followed by her three precious cubs.
They quickly disappeared into a plethora of shrubs.

THE MOUNTAIN LIONS

Jack went barking after the little mountain lions.
After Bill's yell, Jack stopped in a patch of dandelions.

The cubs escaped to the safety of their mother.
They huddled close to being near one another.

Bill went back to the tractor, plowing the field.
This good farmer strived for a bumper wheat yield.

Aunt Susie brought out supper for them to eat.
They had sandwiches with cheese and liverwurst meat.

THE BIRTHDAY PARTY

Jack's birthday entertainment was an acrobat.
They invited the pig, horse, cow, chicken, and a cat.

Jack's presents included a leather collar.
On the buckle was a glistening silver dollar.

His birthday party was a smashing success.
The pig oinked, the horse whinnied, the cow mooed; oh yes.

The cat meowed, the chicken clucked, and Jack did bark.
In their own language, each animal had a happy remark.

TRI-POD

The next day, Bill and Jack stopped working to take a break.
They enjoyed two pieces of leftover birthday cake.

Soon, an orphan three-legged dog walked into the farm.
They named him Tri-pod. This misfit was full of charm.

Jack and Bill loved Tri-pod, and he loved them back.
Tri-pod was fun. Enthusiasm he did not lack.

Bill let him ride on Isabel's fender.
Tri-pod needed food. He was very slender.

TO THE GROCERY STORE

Bill took the two dogs to the grocery store to buy food.
The cow also wanted to go, and she mooed.

The dogs picked out T-bone steaks from the butcher shop.
The cow ravaged the vegetable counter nonstop.

While in town, everyone went to the picture show.
The movie was about farm animals, wouldn't you know.

Bill, two dogs, and the cow rode home in the pickup truck.
On the way, they picked up a green hitchhiking duck.

THE HITCHHIKING DUCK

When Aunt Susie saw this group arrive, she laughed.
Her giggle sounded like a low-flying aircraft.

The laughter was contagious, and they couldn't stop.
Finally, everyone swallowed a cough drop.

This seemed to calm things down for the exhausted group.
Aunt Susie fixed a large kettle of vegetable soup.

The hitchhiking duck didn't like it, and he quacked.
Susie got her feelings hurt, so the duck she smacked.

THE MAGNIFICENT FRIENDS

Everyone on the farm had become magnificent friends.
This fantastic menagerie of odds and ends.

The group had learned to help each other in time of need.
They learned how to grow wheat from a tiny seed.

Farmers around the world grow food to feed the hungry.
Some farmers live in the city, but most live in the country.

Mr. Farmer Bill says to stick around and
help with the chores tonight.
If you like chores, he will see you again at daylight.

James Douglas Leach standing on the steps of the
Supreme Court in Washington, D.C.

www.ingramcontent.com/pod-product-compliance
Lightning Source LLC
Chambersburg PA
CBHW041241300726
48978CB00014B/1309